D0941778

Ghoul School

Kevin O'Malley

Ghoul School
Written & Illustrated by Kevin O'Malley

we jump in puddles

Guilford, Connecticut

Published by Muddy Boots
MuddyBootsBooks.com
An imprint of The Rowman & Littlefield Publishing Group, Inc.
4501 Forbes Blvd., Ste. 200, Lanham, MD 20706
www.rowman.com

Distributed by NATIONAL BOOK NETWORK

British Library Cataloguing-in-Publication Information available

Library of Congress Control Number: 2018942116
ISBN 978-1-63076-3374 (hardcover)
ISBN 978-1-63076-3381 (e-book)

∞™ The paper used in this publication meets the minimum requirements of American National Standard for Information Sciences–Permanence of Paper for Printed Library Materials, ANSI/NISO Z39.48-1992.

"For my beautiful and charming grandson Cameron.
Welcome to the world." –KO

My name is Bea A. Fraid and I go to an
all Ghoul School.

At my school everybody is taught to do scary stuff. We learn how to make a haunted house and paint terrifying pictures.

There are classes in screaming like a lunatic, BOOO-ing, and scaring people in graveyards.

The very best students in Ghoul School are the scariest.
I guess I like my school okay, but, the thing is, I don't really like being scary. I think it is sort of boring. I prefer to laugh.

My art teacher, Ms. Ivana Suckublood, said, "You really must try harder, Bea. Your grades are getting worse and worse." I got a C– in scary pumpkin carving.

I give it my best shot, but I'm just not that good at it. One time I danced down the hallway snapping my fingers.

Mr. Tombstone said, "What are you doing, Bea?"

"I'm doing the Boogie-man!"

Some kids looked pretty scared. I guess I'm not a very good dancer.

I had to go see the principal, Mrs. Ima Grave. "Bea," she said, "I don't know what I'm going to do with you. This is a Ghoul School for goodness' sake. You really must try harder to be scary."

I tried. I really did. But most days I found being scary was funny.

On the way to school I said, "ARRRRR . . . . what does a Frankenstein wear when it's raining?

GHHHHOOOUUUULL-oshes!"
Ghouls ran to get away from me.

9

At lunch I put on my best scary face and said,
"What is a vampire's favorite soup?
SCREAM OF TOMATO!"

I laughed so hard milk came out of my nose.
Some ghouls picked up their trays and ran out
of the cafeteria.

At recess I growled and said, "What does a werewolf say when he sits on sandpaper? **RUFF!**"
I cracked up.

The ghouls in my class hid behind the bushes.
Truth is, everybody was starting to get a little
nervous around me.

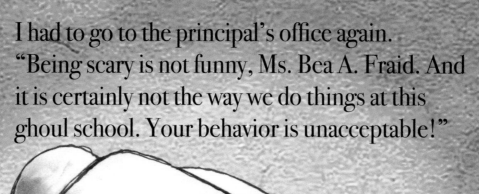

I had to go to the principal's office again.
"Being scary is not funny, Ms. Bea A. Fraid. And
it is certainly not the way we do things at this
ghoul school. Your behavior is unacceptable!"

I couldn't help myself. The more I looked at ghouls trying to be scary, the funnier I thought they were.

Three witches were crying out: "Boil, boil, toil, and trouble!" I laughed and said, "Is it true that a witch on a beach is called a sandwich?"

The witches looked more than a little scared.

A vampire ghoul jumped out and tried to scare me.
I laughed and said, "Let me get you some
mouthwash...you have bat breath."
He ran screaming down the hall.

A ghost flew up and twirled around me.
"Booooo," he moaned.
I laughed and said, "Let me get you a tissue. I can see a boo-ger in your nose."
He looked downright scared. Maybe my jokes aren't that funny.

A zombie staggered up to me and moaned:
"Brains! I want brains!"
I laughed and said, "Well, you don't want me.
I'm a comedian—I taste funny."
He looked like he was going to cry.

Back to the principal's office I went.
"Bea A. Fraid, what you are doing is not funny.
Your behavior is scaring the other students."
That's when I figured it out.
"Wait a minute," I giggled. "If every ghoul in
school is scared because I tell jokes, that would
mean I'm the scariest ghoul in school, right?"

I laughed so hard I almost fell out of my chair.

I couldn't stop laughing.
Mrs. Ima Grave looked pretty nervous. She said,
"Being scary is not funny!"
I couldn't help myself. I said, "What
kind of hot dogs do ghouls like best?
Halloweiners!"
Mrs. Grave screamed,
"Funny is scary!"

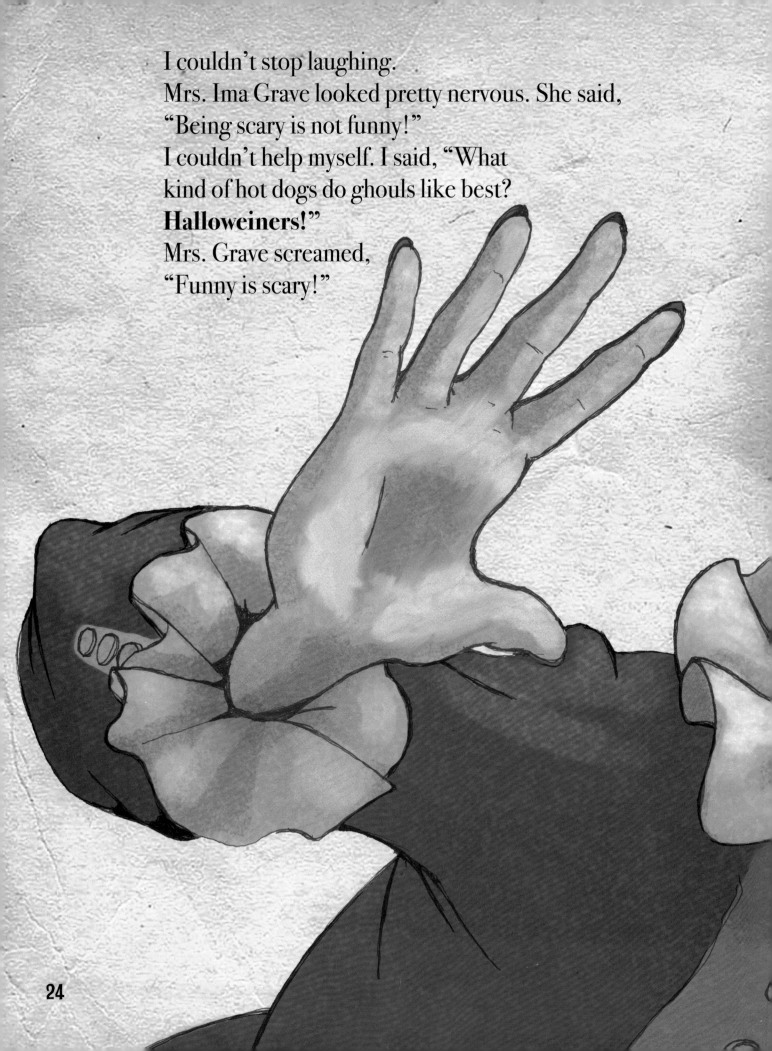

She ran out of the
office. I never saw
her again.

I'm still the scariest ghoul at school, but I won't be for long. Other ghouls are catching on to making jokes. Just the other day, three of my zombie friends staggered down the hallway.

The first one moaned,
"I Scream!"
The second one groaned,
"You Scream!"

And the third ghoul said,

"We all Scream for ICE CREAM!"

Frankenstein laughed so hard he went to pieces.